This book belongs to

_____

Published by Advance Publishers
© 1998 Disney Enterprises, Inc.
All rights reserved. Printed in the United States.
No part of this book may be reproduced or copied in any form
without the written permission of the copyright owner.

Written by Lisa Ann Marsoli
Illustrated by Arkadia Illustration Ltd.
Produced by Bumpy Slide Books

ISBN: 1-885222-99-8

10 9 8 7 6 5 4 3 2 1

Jasmine threw open a window and looked out onto another clear, bright morning in Agrabah. "Aladdin," she said, "where should we go today?"

Jasmine had spent so many years behind the palace walls that she was always ready to see someplace new.

"Why don't we just hop on the Magic Carpet and let him decide?" Aladdin suggested.

Soon the happy couple and Abu were soaring above the city and out over the endless desert. Suddenly the earth below rumbled, and the figure of a giant tiger emerged from the sand.

"That's odd," said Aladdin as the carpet zoomed them in for a closer look. "The Cave of Wonders doesn't appear just any old time. Something strange must be going on in there!"

"Well, I was hoping for an adventure today," answered Jasmine with a grin. "So why don't we take a look! What do you say, Abu? Abu?"

Abu remembered what had happened the last

time he and Aladdin were in the Cave of Wonders — and he was not anxious to go back! So he was hiding underneath the carpet, hoping Jasmine and Aladdin would go on without him.

"No way, Abu!" Aladdin said, scooping up his
pet. "Where we go, you go!"

The trio walked cautiously through the mouth of the tiger. Nothing happened. "So far, so good," Jasmine said with relief. But as they walked farther, they heard a loud clattering echo through the cave.

Abu jumped on top of Aladdin's head and hid, trembling, under his friend's hat. "I think it's coming from the Treasure Room," Aladdin said, grabbing Jasmine's hand. "Quick! This way!"

Jasmine gasped as they neared the entrance to the chamber. Inside, an idol encrusted with emeralds, rubies, and sapphires glittered by the light of the torch Aladdin carried.

"Amazing, isn't it?" asked Aladdin. "When Abu and I first came here —"

But before Aladdin could finish, something crashed to the floor in front of him.

"Look!" shouted Jasmine. "It's a lamp!"

"And a noisy one at that!" noticed Aladdin as the lamp bounced from one wall to the next, crashing into everything in its path.

When the lamp finally stopped bouncing,
Aladdin took a closer look.
"There's something awfully familiar about this
lamp," Aladdin said. Abu nodded vigorously.

Jasmine picked up the lamp. "Well, it does look like the kind genies live in — but do all magic lamps look the same?" she wondered.

The booming voice of the Cave of Wonders interrupted them. "Take the lamp from this cave so that peace may reign here once more!" it commanded.

"I think we'd better listen," warned Aladdin.

"Abu didn't do what it said last time, and we were almost buried alive!"

Just then, the lamp leapt out of Jasmine's hands.

"I just don't see how we're going to be able to catch that thing," said Aladdin.

"Step aside," commanded Jasmine. She took a scarf from her waist and whipped it around over her head. Within seconds, she had lassoed the

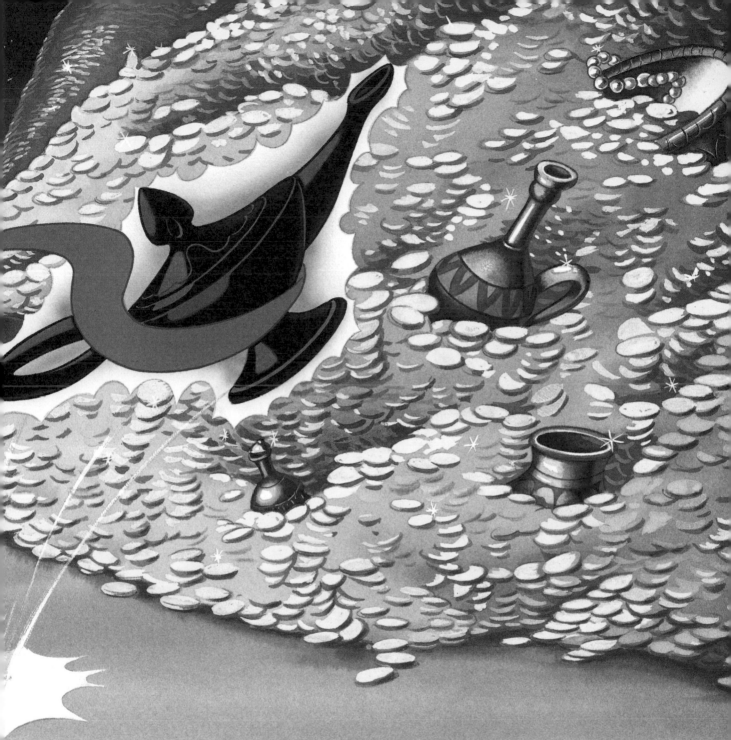

bouncing lamp. Jasmine turned and smiled at Abu
and Aladdin. "Ready to go?" she asked, hopping
up on the Magic Carpet.

"Wow!" Aladdin said admiringly. "You bet!"

Back at the palace, the lamp continued its wild
bouncing. Rajah thought it was a kind of game, and
swiped at it each time it flew by.

"I'd really like to know what's in there,"
Jasmine said. "But I'm afraid to rub it."

"I know what you mean," agreed Al. "I wish
the Genie were here. He'd know what to do."

"You called?" asked the Genie, flying in through an open window.

The old friends greeted each other, and Aladdin explained their dilemma.

"C'mon, Al, where's your sense of adventure?
Let's rub the lamp — how bad could it be?" the
Genie asked.

"Wow! Really, really bad," the Genie admitted.
There, before their very eyes, was — Jafar!

"Well, Al," said the Genie, "it looks as if this is
the same lamp I pitched into the Cave of Wonders.

But hey! This could be a good thing, because I
guess now *I'm* this big guy's —"
  "Master!" shouted Jasmine and Aladdin.

"So what is your first wish?" Jafar snarled at
the Genie. "Stop torturing me and let's get this
joyous little reunion over with!"

But torturing Jafar was exactly what the Genie had in mind — and what better way than by making Jafar do good deeds? Jafar hated good deeds more than anything!

So the Genie's first wish was that Jafar go out among the poor children of Agrabah and distribute food, money, and clothing.

The children could hardly believe their eyes,
and showered Jafar with thanks and praise. When
at last Jafar finished his mission, he returned to the
palace with relief. Being kind had given him a
genie-sized headache!

For his second wish, the Genie commanded Jafar to feed and bathe every animal in the menagerie.

That included brushing Rajah's coat and filing his
nails. Jafar fumed as Aladdin, Jasmine, Abu, and the
Genie looked on with huge grins on their faces.

"Oh, Jafar!" called Jasmine. "I think you missed
a spot behind Rajah's ear!"

After Jafar had finished, the Genie turned into a schoolteacher and asked, "What have we learned today, Jafar?"

"That if you're as rotten as I am, goodie-goodies like you can make life a misery! Now make your third wish, already!"

"Oh, dear," said the Genie, pretending to be upset. "I think you need an attitude adjustment!"

Aladdin and Jasmine moved in closer. "What are
you going to wish last?" asked Aladdin.
"Yes, I can't stand the suspense!" Jasmine added.

"My final wish, Jafar," proclaimed the Genie, "is that one day, when you least expect it, you will become a goodie-goodie, too!" A little shudder ran through Jafar.

"Anything but that!" he yelled as he disappeared back into the lamp.

The Genie picked up the lamp and wound up like
a baseball pitcher. "Now, I want you to go to your
room and think about what I've said," he instructed
as he threw the lamp back to the Cave of Wonders.

"See you later!" called Aladdin.
"Much, much later," Jasmine added with a laugh.

"Do you think Jafar will ever give up his rotten ways?" asked Aladdin.

"I don't know," said the Genie. "Doing the right thing comes naturally to some people. But with Jafar, it may take ten thousand years or so!"

Jafar sat in his magic lamp
Waiting for a master,
But when he saw just who it was,
He thought, "What a disaster!"
The Genie wished Jafar
To change forever and behave,
But he remained a meanie
And was sent back to his cave!